W
Walker, Anna.
I love my dad /
~~53372082852776~~

D0431765

WITHDRAWN

WORN, SOILED, OBSOLETE

For Scott — a great dad

SIMON & SCHUSTER BOOKS FOR YOUNG READERS

An imprint of Simon & Schuster Children's Publishing Division

1230 Avenue of the Americas, New York, New York 10020

Text and illustrations copyright © 2009 by Anna Walker

First published in Australia in 2009 by Scholastic Press

Published by arrangement with Scholastic Australia Pty Limited

First U.S. edition 2010

All rights reserved, including the right of reproduction in whole
or in part in any form.

SIMON & SCHUSTER BOOKS FOR YOUNG READERS is a trademark
of Simon & Schuster, Inc.

For information about special discounts for bulk purchases, please contact
Simon & Schuster Special Sales at 1-866-506-1949 or
business@simonandschuster.com.

The Simon & Schuster Speakers Bureau can bring authors to your live event.
For more information or to book an event,
contact the Simon & Schuster Speakers Bureau at
1-866-248-3049 or visit our website at www.simonspeakers.com.

The text for this book is handwritten by Anna Walker.

The illustrations for this book are rendered in ink on watercolor paper.

Manufactured in Singapore

10 9 8 7 6 5 4 3 2 1

CIP data for this book is available from the Library of Congress.

ISBN 978-1-4169-8319-4

I Love My Dad

by Anna Walker

SIMON & SCHUSTER BOOKS FOR YOUNG READERS

New York • London • Toronto • Sydney

My name is Ollie.

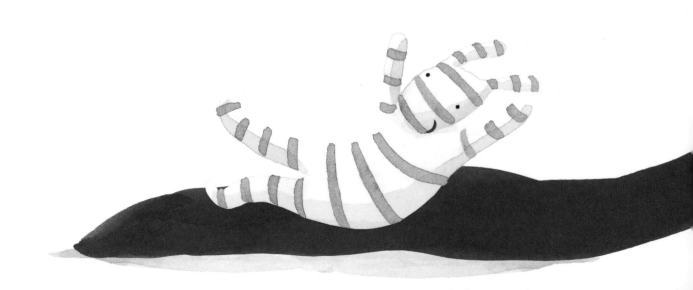

I love my dad.

We make banana bread—
yum yum!

Hot cocoa for everyone.

I ride my bike.

"Dad, look at me!"

We go to the park

and climb the tree.

I love to swing high,

and touch the sky.

When Dad's painting,

I paint too.

I love to hide and then
shout "Boo!"

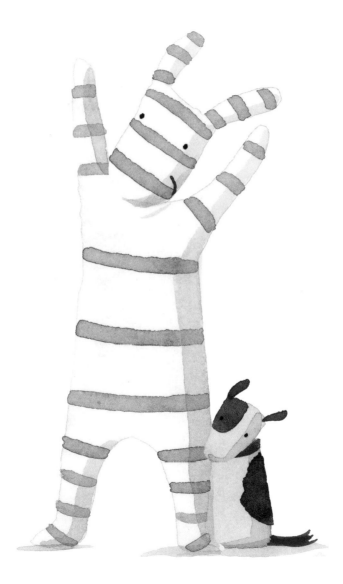

But what I love best
is my piggyback to bed.
I love my dad.
Sweet dreams, Fred.